Gordon's Porch
Two

David R. Beshears

Literary Fiction
Part Two of Serial

Greybeard Publishing
Washington State

Greybeard Publishing
P.O. Box 480
McCleary, WA 98557-0480

ISBN 978-0-9987535-6-0

Gordon's Porch

Two

Chapter One

Thirteen modest homes lined the quiet side-street, six houses on one side, seven on the other. The neighborhood saw very little traffic, which allowed the neighborhood's mostly elderly residents to take their walks down the center of the road with little fear of getting run over.

On days such as this day, with the air being cool without being cold, the sky partly cloudy without being gray, Gordon would often take a morning stroll up and down the street. James sometimes walked with him, as he was doing this day. James had recently begun using a cane, more for his own reassurance than of necessity, as his left knee on occasion had a mind of its own.

They walked as far as Annie's house, the last house on the left. They gave a wave when they saw her standing at her window, coffee cup in hand. They turned about then and started back. Halfway back to Gordon's, they hesitated in front of Kate's home. There was a *for sale* sign in the yard.

Kate, had been a petite woman somewhere in her mid-eighties, had lived alone since her husband had lost his battle with cancer two years earlier. She had never really gotten over losing Richard, and had refused to leave the home that they had bought together a lifetime ago. She hadn't been all that well herself of late, and so had been visited regularly by home-care.

Her nurse had found her in her bed, where she had passed away in her sleep.

"A helluva neighborhood." James was leaning heavily over his cane, looking beyond the *for sale* sign to the small house. It somehow looked sad, lonely. "We might as well be living in an old folks home."

Gordon had heard that comment from James more than once recently. He looked down the street at the well cared for homes that made up their neighborhood.

"When you're surrounded by old people, you're gonna see a lot more dying than regular people face."

"Kinda my point," said James.

Continuing to look down the street, Gordon saw Carol's car backing out of his driveway. His daughter was heading off the work. Her schedule fluctuated and Gordon was never quite sure what her hours were one day to the next.

James gave a nod in the general direction of the retreating vehicle and they started walking again.

"How's Carol liking her new job?" he asked.

"Fine, I suppose. She's not saying much one way or the other."

"That doesn't sound like Carol," said James.

Carol had taken an administration position at the nearby hospital, giving her a lot shorter commute than her last job. She had been looking for something closer since moving in with her dad a few months earlier, and then this position opened up, a perfect fit for her.

"I know," said Gordon. *Should I say anything, or keep my mouth shut?* "I think she might be seeing someone," he said at last.

"Really?"

"She's been spending more time away from home the last couple of weeks. Beyond her work hours, I mean." *Whatever those are...*

"I see." A smarmy smile slowly formed on James' face. "Will a rich doctor soon be joining the family?"

I knew I shouldn't have said anything...

They reached Gordon's and started across the yard to the porch. James used his cane for balance as he carefully took the steps, went over to his chair at the end of the row and sat down with a tired groan. Gordon went inside the house, came out a minute later with two coffee cups. He handed one to James and sat down in his chair on the other side of the small side-table.

"Kate and Richard," Gordon started casually. "Remember? They were the very first of us in the neighborhood."

"I remember," said James, matter-of-factly.

"The very first in the brand new neighborhood. They bought their place about a month before Jan and I moved in."

"I remember."

"Their first home. Only home," Gordon took a sip of his coffee. "Ours, too. Jan and me."

James gave a nostalgic smile.

"Jan brought homemade cookies over the day Naomi and I moved in," he said.

"God, we were all so young then."

James gave a sigh at that, looking out at the neighborhood. Their neighborhood.

"Surprising, really, how many of us are still here," he said. "Although we're a helluva lot greyer."

"We have lost a few," said Gordon, after a long moment.

They fell quiet then. They drank their coffee, hands wrapped about the warm ceramic cups.

"Changes are coming to the old neighborhood," said James then. "New folks'll be moving in."

"It had to happen," said Gordon. *Losing the old crowd...*

Another long pause then.

James took another swallow of his coffee.

"My God, those cookies were awful."

§

Miss McCarthy came out onto her front porch, stepped to one side so that Rocky could scurry past. She closed the door then and followed her collie down onto the front yard.

The elderly woman, as stout and as strong-willed as ever, was doing quite well after her earlier health scare. She had chased the home-care nurse off long ago.

She watched Rocky scamper about the yard, visiting all his favorite spots. The old dog looked back occasionally, making sure that the woman was still there.

Miss McCarthy gave Rocky a warm, reassuring smile and the collie continued about his business.

The old woman had been alone for half her life, all but for the last ten years with Rocky.

Sensing movement, she looked out at the street.

Lloyd Weaver was taking his morning walk, his tall wooden staff in hand. The old gentleman was somewhere between seventy-five and a hundred and five years old, thin and bony and grey and scruffy, his appearance unchanged in the last thirty years as far as anyone could tell.

Miss McCarthy offered him a friendly hello. He gave a silent acknowledgment in reply and continued past. Miss McCarthy went to her garden hose then and turned on the faucet. It was time to wash away Rocky's leavings.

Gordon and James were still on the porch, enjoying their morning coffee. James gave a nod in the direction of the street. Lloyd Weaver was walking past. When they spotted Lloyd giving them a furtive side-glance, Gordon lifted his coffee cup in a silent hello.

Lloyd Weaver briefly held out his tall, wooden staff in reply and then continued silently past.

"Another of our neighborhood's founding members," said James.

A long pause, and then Gordon offered James more coffee.

"No, I'm good," said James.

A few moments later, and then Rocky made his own daily appearance, working his way from yard to yard across the street, taking care of business.

Gordon and James were much comforted by the sight of the old dog – *the world is still here...*

Chapter Two

The day was cool and gray. Annie was sitting in the third chair in the row of four chairs that were lined up on Gordon's porch, wearing a warm flannel shirt under a light jacket, holding a cup of hot tea in both hands.

The third chair from the end was her chair.

Gordon was sitting quietly in his own chair, the second from the end, dressed in a thick sweater. He doubted the sun would ever burn through the low clouds. How quickly the weather changed one day to the next, particularly this time of year.

He leaned over and picked up the thermos that was sitting on the side-table, offered to replenish Annie's tea with a gesture. She shook her head no and placed a hand over her cup.

Gordon refilled his own cup, set the thermos back on the table and slid back in his chair.

"I doubt we'll be seeing any sunshine today," he said. "A sure sign that Thanksgiving will soon be here."

"The holidays are coming with increased rapidity," she said. "I don't like that."

"A cruel irony, Annie," said Gordon. "The older you get, the faster the years go by."

They saw then James coming up the street. Reaching Gordon's, he started across the yard, cane in one hand, travel mug in the other. He worked his way up the steps and walked past his friends. He leaned his cane against the rail and dropped into his chair at the end of the row.

He adjusted the knit cap on his head.

"I believe it's about time to break out the porch heater, Gordon," he said.

"If only I had one of those."

"Right," droned James. "I'll have John bring one of mine over."

James' son John dropped by to see James at least twice a week. In addition to a pleasant visit, and a chance to make sure Dad was well and good, there was usually a chore or two that needed doing.

The talk of bringing over one of James' porch heaters came up every year about this time.

"You can if you like," said Gordon. "But you'll be needing them all yourself, come Thanksgiving."

This also was mentioned every year about this time.

Thanksgiving was usually celebrated in James' back yard, taking advantage of his expansive deck and well-manicured back lawn. It was tradition, really, a neighborhood celebration. And the porch heaters were a common sight at these events. And should it rain, canopies were sometimes raised.

Quite strange, though, that while Thanksgiving day was often cool in the neighborhood, it almost never rained. The day before, perhaps, and maybe the day after, but almost never on Thanksgiving Day itself.

"Remember the holidays growing up?" asked Gordon, nostalgically, a smile from the memories. "Thanksgiving, Christmas, Fourth of July."

"Sure, sure," said James.

"The gatherings at Grandma's, all the families getting together," said Gordon, his words fading then, lost in thought. Gordon had lived with his grandparents off and on when growing up. And those had been special times, those holiday gatherings.

"Same here," said Annie. "Big get-together at my grandparents' every Thanksgiving. All the aunts and uncles and cousins. Then Abuelita passed away, and after that the families all drifted apart; everyone started doing their own thing."

A long pause, all three looking out at the neighborhood, drinking their hot tea.

They had told each other these stories a dozen times or more over the years.

"That's just the way of things," said James.

Another long pause. "Still sucks," said Annie.

"Yeah," said James and Gordon at the same time.

Silence on the porch, a heavy quiet across the neighborhood.

A car came onto their street then, disturbing that quiet.

Carol was coming home. She pulled the car into the driveway.

"Kinda early for Carol to be coming home, isn't it?" asked James.

"Depends on the day of the week," said Gordon. "Today's a short day. Or maybe it's an off day. Don't remember."

"Ah," James said, broad smile. "Perhaps she was visiting a friend."

Gordon said nothing.

James gave his brow a wiggle.

"What's this about, then?" asked Annie.

"Nothing," said Gordon, a bit too sharply.

Carol stepped up onto the porch. She leaned against a post and crossed her arms, a small, white paper bag in one hand. She had been to the pharmacy, had picked up her dad's prescription.

"So, how go things with the Hole in the Wall Gang?" she asked the group.

"Well enough, young lady," said James. "How 'bout yourself? How go things with you? The new job? Work mates?"

"Well enough," said Carol, hint of a smile.

It looked like that was all James was going to get from her. Carol looked to Gordon and held up the small, paper bag. Gordon nodded a thank you and Carol pushed off the post then and started toward the door.

"Does anyone need anything?" she asked.

"Warmer weather?" suggested James.

"I'll see what we have in the fridge," said Carol, opening the door.

James managed a grunt at that as Carol disappeared inside.

"Not to complain," said Gordon then, focusing again out at the neighborhood, "but since Carol moved in, I think I've gone to the grocery store like once, maybe twice."

"Yeah?" said James, offhandedly. "So?"

Gordon gave another of his tired sighs, shrugged.

"Nothing, I guess," he said. "Just, I used to go every week. Now, I check the pantry, the freezer, the fridge, looking to make my shopping list. Pantry's full, freezer's full. Fridge." Another shrug.

"Uh, huh," James said, quite matter-of-factly. "And so you are deprived from going to the grocery store."

"Well... yeah."

"I struggle to hold back the tears."

"I shop online," Annie stated frankly. "Groceries delivered."

"We know," said Gordon. "But you don't drive."

"Still," she said. "I like it."

"I know."

The three continued to look out across the yard, to the street, the neighborhood.

"I'm sure Carol asks you if you need anything," said Annie. "Right?"

"Well, yeah."

"So, I'm sure she that sees it as taking the shopping chore off your shoulders."

James considered Annie's observation, then had an observation of his own for Gordon.

"Jan used to do the shopping, didn't she?" he asked.

"Well, yeah."

"So you're bitching just to bitch. Aren't you?"

"Well, yeah."

They all managed slight smiles, almost smirking, almost but not quite snickering.

"It sure is chilly out," said Annie, after a long while.

"Yeah," sighed Gordon. "Chilly."

"Yeah," said James. "Thanksgiving coming up."

Chapter Three

Carol opened the door and went into her dad's bedroom to collect his laundry basket. Collecting his laundry basket was the only circumstance in which she was allowed into his room. Laundry was one of the house chores that her dad had readily allowed Carol to take over from him. The issue of the laundry was apparently a sensitive matter of her dad's.

It had something to do with laundry soap pods.

She picked up the basket that was sitting next to the dresser. On her way out she noted the pajama bottoms that were hanging on the wall next to the door. Her dad didn't wear pajamas to bed, but since Carol had moved back home he kept them at the ready should he need to get up during the night; a more and more frequent occurrence and he didn't want to be caught in the hallway in his underwear.

She briefly considered including them in the laundry but thought better of it and left the bedroom without the pajama bottoms, closing the door on the way out. Walking down the hall, she passed the closed door to her dad's office.

Door closed, so off limits, at least without knocking first and receiving a come on in greeting. He had been spending more time in there of late. He had begun working on something and wasn't yet ready to let her in on what it was.

Expect he'll let me know what it is once he's ready.

§

Gordon and Carol had finished lunch and Gordon had gone out onto the porch, where he was enjoying an after-meal ginger peach tea. Good for the digestion, so he had heard.

It was almost pleasant out. The afternoon was a bit warmer than the past few days, and the sun was actually out. He was wearing a light windbreaker against the occasional breeze.

He absently watched James make his way slowly up the street, across the lawn, and finally awkwardly up the steps. Gordon silently noted that his friend appeared to be relying his cane more and more.

"Coffee? Tea?" Gordon asked, once James had settled into his chair.

James shook his head no, commented then that he was done with coffee for the day.

"Water then? A slice of lemon?"

James gave another negative shake of the head.

The conversation drifted to the almost pleasant day, what with the sun making an appearance and all. James said that he was planning to take advantage of the weather to do some work in his back yard later.

The front door opened and Carol rushed out in a panic. She hurried across the porch and leapt past the steps to the yard below, calling back over her shoulder.

"Call 911! Call 911! Annie! Hurt! Ambulance!"

"What?!" Gordon jumped to his feet, calling out to Carol as she rushed across the yard.

"Ambulance! Annie's!" Carol called out loudly back over her shoulder.

And then she was in the street, running up the street.

James stood beside Gordon, the two watching Carol running headlong toward Annie's.

"Well?" James to Gordon.

"Right," said Gordon, turning to the door. "911."

§

The gurney took up much of Annie's living room. Carol was standing beside the gurney, holding Annie's hand. Annie's expression was more one of embarrassment than of pain or discomfort.

Annie's body was secured to prevent movement, and her forehead had been bandaged.

"I'll be right behind you," said Carol.

Annie gave a nod and a thin smile in answer. She looked over at Gordon and James, who were standing well out of the way. She gave them an awkward wave with her free hand.

The two EMTs wheeled the gurney to the front door and maneuvered it out of the house. Gordon stepped up beside Carol.

"I'm not sure," said Carol, anticipating her dad's question. "She turned wrong, her hip gave out."

"Ouch."

"On her way down, she hit her head on the counter."

"Not good, the hip," James said somberly, stepping up beside them. "Not good. Broke it?"

"I don't know," said Carol. "Maybe not. Maybe tore something."

"She'll be fine," Gordon stated firmly. "She'll be fine."

"Absolutely," agreed James. "They don't come any tougher than our Annie Romero."

Carol frowned, looking at Gordon.

"Dad," she started, sounding a bit accusatory. "She was laying there on the kitchen floor, somehow managed to drag herself to the phone. Does she call 911? No. She doesn't. She calls you."

"Um..." Gordon struggled. What was he to say to that? "I'm sorry?"

Carol's expression turned apologetic.

"No, no. I'm sorry. She was hurt, she called her friend for help." Carol said then, placing a comforting hand on her dad's shoulder. "I'm heading over to the hospital. I'll make sure everything's in order."

"Give me a chance to stop by the house. I'd like to go with you," said Gordon.

"I expect it'll be some time before you can see her. You hold off, I'll give you a call the minute she can have visitors."

Gordon didn't look like he was going to accept that; he looked from Carol to James.

"That sounds best," said James to Gordon. He looked to Carol. "We'll be waiting for your call."

And with that Carol gave her dad a comforting smile and followed after Annie.

They weren't able to get in to see their friend until that evening, and then the visit had been brief. Annie had spent the day going through examinations and tests, a trip to the OR, more time in recovery, finally then getting settled into her room.

She hadn't exactly been up to an extended visit.

The next day had been better, the day after that even better.

James was standing in the street in front of Kate's house, leaning over his cane.

The "*for sale*" sign in the yard now had a "sold" sticker on it. There were two cars in the driveway and James could see movement in the house through the windows.

Gordon approached from the direction of Annie's house.

"What's up?" he asked.

"Sold, looks like," said James.

"Yeah, I saw," said Gordon, looking toward the house. "The new neighbors?"

"Don't know. Probably," James shrugged. "Young folks, I think."

Gordon nodded, took a moment, studying the uncurtained windows and watching for signs of those *young folks* of which James spoke.

"Checking their new digs, you think? Measuring for the furniture?"

"Can't tell," said James. He looked to Gordon, then up the street. "Checking on Annie's place?"

"She asked me to look in, water her plants."

"Right." James gave a nod, watched then as a young couple came out of the newly sold house and started toward one of the vehicles, soon followed by a slightly older couple.

James turned away then and he and Gordon started walking down the street.

"Tomorrow, then?" he asked Gordon, about Annie coming home.

"That's the word."

"Good sign," said James. "Six days, though. She's gotta be going nuts about now. I know I would be."

"Yeah, well... it could've been worse."

"S'pose that's so," agreed James.

Annie hadn't broken her hip, rather had torn something or other when she had turned wrong. She had recovery and therapy ahead, but yes, it could have been much worse.

And she had friends to help...

"We'll soon have her back to fighting trim," said James.

"We'll have a hard time holding her back."

"True enough," said James. "Which means that targeting our assistance won't be easy."

"That's kind of where I'm going." Gordon recalled his most recent visit to see Annie. "You know, listening to her, there's nothing wrong with her, she's fine. She's just fine."

"That's Annie, all right," said James. "So, we work around the edges, handle chores before she does. We can't do much more than that."

A few easy paces in the quiet of the neighborhood, and James gave a nostalgic *hmmm...*

"What's that?" asked Gordon.

"Oh, nothing really." James tapped his cane on the street, they strode a few more steps. "Just thinking about Naomi."

Gordon gave his own nostalgic *hmmm...* at that.

"I loved her dearly," said James. "Life would've been so much less without her," he said, memories flooding in. "I miss her so."

"A great lady, all right."

"That she was. Naomi was..." Hesitation. "But..."

"But what?"

"Well... with Naomi, for Naomi, a sniffle was always pneumonia. Right? Aches and pains were always crippling, she wasn't gonna make it through the day. Cold days were Arctic winters, hot days were spent wandering the Sahara."

Yep, thought Gordon. *That had been Naomi, all right.*

Their pace had slowed, memories were coming at them from the past. Gordon struggled to hold back the nostalgic smile.

James went on then.

"Now, Naomi did have serious health issues. Real issues. That's a fact, God bless her," he said. "So... the way I had to address those very real issues, those serious issues, I had to filter out all the extraneous to get to them."

"I get that," said Gordon, just above a whisper.

"Not always easy. Right?" James went on. "Sometimes, well, it could be exhausting."

They fell silent then, their pace still slow. Gordon's place was still a ways up ahead. Gordon's thoughts drifted back to the long Summer days on the porch, way back when.

James looked side-glance at his friend.

"What are you smiling at, Gordon?" he asked, the tone almost an accusation.

"Am I smiling?" he asked. "I don't know, really."

A few more steps, only the wooden click of James' cane on the asphalt breaking the quiet of the neighborhood.

"I miss her too," said Gordon then.

Silent then, the rest of the way to Gordon's porch.

Chapter Four

Gordon leaned back in his desk chair and stared at the computer monitor. He frowned at the screen of text, looked briefly away, looked over at his small office's one small window. The curtains were pulled aside, allowing the slowly brightening morning gray to shine through.

He glanced over at the wall clock then. He was about finished with the morning's writing session, but there was still some time before he was to head over to James' house.

His desk chair squeaked painfully as he leaned forward. He rolled the computer mouse across the pad, aimed the cursor and closed out the word processing application. He reached out then and turned off the monitor. He stood up, pushed the chair under the desk and left his office.

The house was quiet. This was one of Carol's long work days and she had left for the hospital about the time the sun was coming up.

Gordon decided to do a few chores, not that his daughter ever left much for him to do. He took the carpet sweeper out of the hall closet and went from room to room, rolled the sweeper back and forth over the room rugs. That done, he went into the kitchen, emptied the dishwasher.

Looking about then for something else to do, he finally reheated a cup of cold coffee in the microwave and stepped out onto the porch. He stood at the top step, drank his coffee and watched for the sun to finish burning off the gray.

He looked down at his watch.

If he took a slow walk around the neighborhood, he would get to James' place just about right on time.

Gordon stood with James on his friend's back deck. They had finished going over their plans for the neighborhood Thanksgiving celebration, now just two days away. The expansive back deck was ready, the lawn and greenery were all trimmed and ready to go. And James' son John had been doing a bit of landscaping work over the last few weeks as he had time.

And it now looked like the weather was going to be in their favor again this year... partly cloudy, perhaps a bit warmer than normal.

Today was a bit damp from a brief overnight shower and morning gray skies, but the extended forecast said no more rain at least through the weekend, maybe longer.

"Should be great this year," said Gordon, probably for the fourth time that morning.

"Yep," said James. He folded his arms across his chest, gave a nod to the yard. Just about everyone in the neighborhood would be gathering for the celebration. "Really too bad about Annie, though. I don't see how she'll be able to make it."

Gordon agreed. Annie was doing well enough, better than expected, but certainly wouldn't be up to a Thanksgiving neighborhood bash.

"I'll talk to her. Maybe we can see about doing something special for her," said Gordon. He would be seeing her in the afternoon. "Nothing demanding, nothing that would set her back."

"Sounds good to me," said James. "Maybe we can just slip out for an hour, head over to visit with her. You and me."

They spent another half hour talking over the plans for the neighborhood celebration, then Gordon left to head home for a quick lunch, after which he went on to Annie's.

He knocked on her front door, opened it and went inside when he heard a *come in* from somewhere in the house. There was no one in the living room, but as he closed the door behind him Annie came hobbling in from the kitchen, pushing a walker in front of her. Carol was right beside her, hovering protectively while keeping hands off.

"Hey, Gordon," said Annie. "Had lunch yet?"

"I'm good, thanks."

Annie reached her chair, shifted carefully about and slowly settled in.

"You sure?" she asked. "Stew ready in a few."

"I'm good." Gordon looked up at his daughter then. "How's she doing, Carol?"

"I do wish she'd take it a little slower, but she's doing well," said Carol. She pulled Annie's walker off to one side but still within Annie's reach. "Great, actually."

"Yeah, she's not one to take things easy."

The injections were done with, Annie now took pain meds only when necessary, and wore a hip brace under her clothes during the day. She was to take short walks several times a day, using a walker and always under the watchful eye of a friend; otherwise she was to rest.

"I'm happy to take things easy." Annie picked up the tv remote and turned on the television. "For the next thirty minutes."

"Right," said Carol. She gave Annie a comforting pat on the shoulder and started toward the door. "I'm off then." To Gordon then, "See you tonight, Dad."

Gordon gave a nod good-bye to Carol, shifted about then and sat in the chair near Annie.

Annie used the remote to change the channel. Music started up from the television's pair of speakers.

It was time for Annie's *story*.

It was her mother's story, actually. It had been her favorite Mexican telenovela.

Gordon watched the story with her, picking up a word here and there but otherwise just watching the program with his friend. He wouldn't be able to talk with her about what to do about Thanksgiving until the day's episode was finished.

James showed up later as Gordon was preparing Annie's lunch tray, this despite her protests, stating quite forcefully that she was perfectly capable of putting her own lunch together. To no avail.

After a short visit, and a promise from Gordon and James that Annie would most definitely not be having Thanksgiving alone, they headed out, started the walk back to Gordon's.

Passing Miss McCarthy's house, they could see Rocky in the window. The drapes were always left open just enough for the dog to stand watch.

Rocky gave a slight tilt of the head, then straightened, neck stiffened, and he fixedly monitored the two men walking down the street past his house.

They continued on down the street and out of sight.

"I don't figure on dying," said Gordon then, a casual toss-off.

"Right," said James. "Good to know. That woulda' ruined the whole day."

"No. I mean not ever."

A few steps in silence.

"Really..." said James, half question, half comment.

"Really. I like it here."

"I see," said James, casually. "Does Carol know about this? You know, she probably had plans for the house."

"Sure. I told her."

"And?"

"And she said thanks for the heads-up. She'll cancel the appointment with the realtor."

Another half-dozen steps nearer Gordon's.

"Good call," said James. "Smart lady."

Chapter Five

Thanksgiving Day... just past noon. Guests had begun arriving about eleven in the morning. James stood now at the edge of the deck, looking from side to side and out at the yard, looking for any last-minute tasks that needed doing.

Most of the neighbors had arrived, were gathered in small groups around snack tables, a few hovering near the heater towers. Several food tables were set up under a pair of canopies.

James' son John and John's wife were out in the yard, making the rounds, moving from guest to guest, asking if anyone needed anything.

Gordon arrived then, coming into the yard from the open side gate. He stepped up onto the deck and walked over to James. He was wearing a light jacket, as the noonday sun had yet to burn through the last of the thinning clouds.

James picked up a thermos from a small table and filled a mug with hot chocolate, handed it to Gordon. Hot chocolate had long ago become a tradition of the annual neighborhood Thanksgiving celebration. There were a number of carafes and thermoses on tables all about the yard.

Gordon took a cautious sip.

"Mmm, good," he said. He glanced about at those on the deck, at those milling about out in the yard. From what he could tell, most everyone was there. Even the young family that lived next door to Gordon;

this was a bit surprising, as they usually spent Thanksgiving with Bob's parents.

Miss McCarthy had even brought Rocky along. The dog was currently drawing the attention of Bob's children.

Carol was scheduled to work through the morning, but had said she would be there soon after noon.

The newest residents to the neighborhood hadn't yet moved in, so maybe next year.

That left only Annie...

Annie wouldn't be coming to the party, so Gordon and James would be taking the party to her.

Well, a bit of the party. A small bit.

But not just yet.

"I do believe it's about time I spread some cheer and joy, James," said Gordon, taking a step nearer the edge of the deck. From the yard came the sound of playful barking. "I can't leave it all to Rocky."

"You do that," said James. He gave a salute with his cup of chocolate. "You go spread that joy, my man."

The sun finished burning away the clouds, scattering bright sunshine all about the yard. The mood among the guests, warm and pleasant before, seemed to shine all the brighter. There was more moving about from group to group, voices cheery.

James came up to Gordon, who had returned to stand on the deck, was looking out at all the activity.

"Everyone looks to be enjoying themselves," said Gordon.

"Glad to see the sun," said James. "I just spoke with John, asked him to keep an eye on things for a bit."

"Right," said Gordon, setting his glass on the side table. "Good a time as any to look in on Annie."

The two of them stepped down from the deck and started toward the gate. Gordon managed to catch Carol's attention, indicated they were leaving.

Carol gave a nod in response.

She would be helping John with hosting duties for the next hour or two.

The walk up the street was eerily quiet. They thought the eeriness odd, as the neighborhood was always quiet, excepting those weekends in the Summer when the sounds of lawnmowers and edgers would shatter the silence. Now, knowing that most of the neighborhood residents were gathered together in James' back yard, that there was no one home, no one on the other side of those front doors, that there would be no shadows moving across those large front windows, the silence was ominous.

Stepping up onto Annie's front porch, Gordon knocked twice, called out that it was Gordon and James, and opened the door. Once inside, they saw that Annie wasn't in the living room.

"Annie?" Gordon called out.

"In here," Annie called back from the kitchen. They found her standing at the counter, her walker set to one side.

"What are you doing?" asked Gordon and James together.

"What does it look like?" She was working on something in a casserole dish, which she had recently taken out of the oven.

It was her special dish, a very special Mexican casserole that she made every Thanksgiving.

"Well... okay, but..." Gordon mumbled, moving up beside her, taking in the aroma.

"What?" snapped Annie. "Do you expect me to just sit there in my chair, twenty-four-seven? I am mobile, you know. There are any number of things I gotta do, like, you know, that I can't do in my chair."

James moved up to stand on the other side of Annie, leaned over and looked down at the casserole. For the moment, he held his silence.

Gordon tried again. "Well... okay, but..." He continued to quite carefully study the casserole. "That does smell good."

Annie slid the dish over to Gordon.

"So, you want to help? Help then." she pushed the oven mitts in his direction.

"Well, all right then," said Gordon. He put on the mitts, picked up the casserole dish and carried it to the table. James was right behind him, leaving Annie to pull the walker over to her and follow after them.

Settling in at the table, Gordon and James noted that silverware and napkins had already been set out. Glasses were filled with iced tea.

Annie maneuvered into her chair, pushed the walker aside. She leaned forward then, gave her guests a broad smile.

"Happy Thanksgiving, you two," she said.

"And to you, Annie," said Gordon.

"Right," said James, reaching for the serving spoon. "Let's eat."

Another key annual activity of Thanksgiving was the day-after cleaning up. James son actually performed much of the clean-up duties the evening before, assigning additional undertakings to his family. But there were always tasks left behind for James and Gordon to tackle the following day.

These they were happy to take on, talking all the while, remarking on the events of the previous day's celebration.

They noted that Miss McCarthy was back to 100%. She had busily worked her way from group to group throughout the celebration, catching up on the gossip and goings-on of the neighborhood. And she had brought Rocky along, the dog as eager as Miss McCarthy to visit with everyone.

It had been great to see Bob's kids at the celebration this year, all the more so to keep Rocky happy.

Lloyd had decorated his tall wooden staff with what he considered to be Thanksgiving-colored streamers, a variety of browns and dark reds. It looked a bit like an off-colored Maypole.

James had hoped that Carol might bring along a friend, the friend she had yet to admit to having, but alas, no. She had come alone.

With the majority of the clean-up duties completed, Gordon repositioned a pair of chairs on the deck as James went into the house, brought out a thermos of coffee and a pair of cups.

Once settled into the chairs, they quietly drank their coffee, admired their work. After some minutes, James looked side-glance to Gordon, looked again out across the yard.

"I sometimes forget things," he said, a bit too casually.

Gordon gave a half smile, frowned then. "Who doesn't?"

James worked his lips, scrunched up his brow.

"Mmm," was all he managed to say.

Another very long pause.

"They have tests for that now," said Gordon. He took another swallow of his coffee.

"Yeah," said James. "I should probably do that."

"Do what?"

"Funny," said James. "Hilarious."

Gordon managed only a half-grin.

They sat quiet for a long time then.

"So..." James started, "Is dementia a form of Alzheimer's, or is it the other way around? And if you say you forget, I'll have to hurt you."

Chapter Six

It had been a long, slow walk.

Annie moved guardedly across Gordon's front yard, pushing her walker forward before her, using it more now as just-in-case security. Gordon and James walked either side beside her. Reaching the steps, Gordon took the walker and held it to one side as he and James supported Annie, helping her take the steps. Once on the porch, they guided her over to her chair. She turned about and eased down into the chair. Gordon positioned the walker within her reach.

"Thank you, gentlemen," she said. She began shifting about, struggling to get comfortable. "Damn hip brace keeps getting in the way."

James moved to his chair at the end of the row. Gordon settled into his own chair between his two companions.

"So how much longer do you have to wear it?" he asked. "The brace."

"I don't have the slightest idea." Annie continued to shift about, finally found a comfortable spot.

"The doctor didn't say?"

"Probably did."

"Probably did?"

"Yup."

"Right," James said finally, after a long pause.

"Annie?" Gordon started. "That might be something you'd want to put on your calendar."

"Yup," she said again. "Might be there."

"Right," said Gordon.

"Right," said James.

They let the conversation drift to silence, all letting the quiet of the neighborhood drift up to the porch.

"It's in the paperwork on the side table in your living room, isn't it?" Gordon asked then.

"Yup," said Annie. "Probably."

"You can be a most irksome lady, Annie."

Annie smiled broadly in answer.

James was done with this. He gave a nod to Rocky. The dog was working his way from yard to yard across the street, from bush to bush, taking care of his business.

"A bit late," he said.

A few moments later, coming down the center of the street, Lloyd Weaver was taking his morning walk. Passing by Gordon's, he briefly lifted his staff in his familiar acknowledgement to those on the porch.

Those on the porch gave brief waves in response.

Rocky was beyond their view now.

Lloyd continued on, passing beyond their view.

The neighborhood again fell quiet.

Gordon looked over at James, then to Annie. He looked out again to the street, to his neighborhood.

"You know," he started then. "I sometimes feel like I'm watching the world from the outside."

"Really," said James, matter-of-factly.

"You?" Gordon prompted.

"Sure," said James. He took a moment, and then, "I suppose that's true for most of us. I mean, our minds are our own after all. Unique; Isolated, really. Except, you know, for those living in gestalt-like cults."

Annie decided to stay out of it for the moment. Gordon and James often went off on wild observations just like this.

"Yeah," said Gordon, considering James' comment. "That's not really where I was going."

"It seldom is," said James, which could have meant anything. Or nothing.

"Weird, I guess." Gordon shrugged. "I guess."

"Yup," said Annie, at last.

"Probably," said James.

Gordon frowned, considered, thought again, considered again.

"It's like..." he started, hesitated. "It's like, I'm not really a part of it. The world I mean."

"Oh, I get that," said James.

"It's like I exist outside of it. I'm separate from it, looking down at it, as an observer."

"You're right, Gordon," said James. "You are weird. I've always said so. Haven't I Annie?"

"Yup," said Annie.

"Yeah." Gordon sighed, frowned again as he looked out at the neighborhood. "More so with Jan gone."

Heavy shadows fell across the porch as clouds began drifting in, passing before the sun.

"Well, that's it then," said James, giving a nod to the vanishing sun. "See you in the Spring."

"Cool breeze," said Annie.

"You want a blanket?" asked Gordon, sliding forward, readying to stand. He did stand then. "Let me get you a blanket."

"That's all right," she said. "I'm all right."

"Too late," said Gordon, standing. "I'm getting you a blanket."

The next day...

A heavy morning mist drifted through the neighborhood, the slight breeze making the morning all the cooler. Gordon, wearing his medium jacket and knit cap, walked down the center of the street, heading home after spending an hour with Annie. He had taken the opportunity to do a few chores as well. If he didn't do them, she would try to do them herself.

He took his time walking home, bundled up in his jacket, his cap pulled down over his ears. He was feeling a bit wistful of late, what with recent events. He wanted to take in the neighborhood.

A wide, quiet street, lined with homes decades old. Modest homes, most with the original owners. These were people he had known most of his adult life. Graying now, as James would say.

Graying...

James always did have a way with the turn of phrase.

Is one word a phrase?

Reaching his home then, he stood out in the street, looking nostalgically at the old house.

This house, this neighborhood, this had been his world for most of his adult life.

His and Jan's.

Sure, they had gone on their annual adventures to amazing places, year after year, but they had always come home... to this house, to this street, to this neighborhood. It had always been here, waiting to welcome them home. Whatever might be *out there*, this was their world. His and Jan's.

Oh, how he missed her; Jan, his life partner.

He started then across the yard. He reached the steps, hesitated a few moments, then took the steps up onto the porch. He looked down the row of four chairs, a small side table between each.

The years spent on Gordon's Porch...

Gordon moved down the row to his chair, the second from the end.

Carol finished up the chores in the kitchen. She moved into the living room, lifted her jacket off the wall hook, slipped into it as she continued to the front door. She grabbed her keys from the tray sitting on the small table beside the door.

Stepping outside, she closed the door and moved across the porch, stood at the top of the steps. She looked back over her shoulder to Gordon, who was sitting in his chair.

"Annie?" she prompted.

"Apparently her hip brace digs at her in all the wrong places," he answered. "Other than that, she's doing a-okay."

Carol chuckled lightly. "I'll have a look at it." She looked out again at the neighborhood.

Lloyd Weaver walking just walking past. The man raised his wooden staff in silent hello. She gave an acknowledging nod and the man continued on his way.

"Dad... where does he go every day?" she asked. "He disappears up the street, and..."

"Lloyd? He goes to that coffee stand over on Parkland. The one with all the benches."

"Mister Weaver going for overpriced morning coffee," said Annie. "Who'd a thought?"

"You remember his daughter? LeeAnne?"

"Sure," said Carol, wondering where this was going. "We went to school together."

"That's the one," said Gordon. "Well, she moved back to town a couple of years ago, set up that coffee stand."

"Ah. So, he's supporting the family enterprise then."

"Maybe," Gordon shrugged. "Maybe he's just getting free coffee. Anyway, he hangs out there, waits for his wife to pick him up. She spends a few hours each morning volunteering at the food bank."

"Wife?" She turned about and gave her dad a questioning look. "I thought he was a widower."

"He was. He remarried. They met at the coffee stand."

"His daughter's coffee stand..."

"Exactly so," said Gordon. He shifted forward slightly, looking out at the street. Lloyd Weaver was already beyond his view, would soon be beyond Carol's line of sight.

As she watched him disappear up the street, she recalled the man's daughter, LeeAnne. She remembered her as being very athletic, strong in sports, as well as being one of the smartest students in the class. She had been one of the first to leave the neighborhood, accepting a college scholarship.

And so the young people had left the neighborhood one by one, with Carol being one of the last to go.

"It's always so quiet here these days," she said. "Without the sound of children playing."

"We do have Bob's children," said Gordon, giving a nod in the direction of his immediate neighbor. The family were rather recent arrivals, moving in some time after Carol had headed off to college and then to her life beyond.

"Too quiet, you ask me."

"Just wait till Spring and the boy brings out the lawn mower."

"That's not what I mean and you know it, Dad." She half-turned then, held up the keys that she'd been holding. "So, I thought I'd do some shopping." She gave her dad a smile and raised a questioning brow.

Gordon hesitated only very briefly, then eased out of his chair with a groan.

"Oh, I guess I could use the distraction," he said.

Chapter Seven

Annie worked her way up the center of the street, pushing her ever-present walker out in front of her. James, relying on his cane more and more, followed along beside her.

She was as yet not allowed to go out on her own.

All part of her therapy.

"Aren't we just a pair?" asked James, waving his cane before him.

"The buddy system," snickered Annie. "I'm here for you if needed."

"Good to know."

They passed Miss McCarthy's, continued to work their way down the street.

"Still," said James. He gave a nod in the general direction of Annie's hip, hidden somewhere beneath the oversized shirt and hidden hip brace. "It could've been worse."

"Yeah, yeah," groaned Annie. *Really gettin' tired of hearing that...*

"Yep. Could've been worse," said James, knowingly, unable to hide the grin.

"Yep," grumbled Annie. *So, so tired. Tired, tired.*

The rest of the way in silence, but for the clicking of Annie's walker at each push forward, and the tapping of James' wooden cane on the asphalt.

Approaching Gordon's, they saw Carol and Gordon taking several bags of groceries out of Carol's car. They continued into the yard, and James stopped, placing a hand on Annie's arm for her to hold up a minute.

"So, Gordon," James called out. "Did she let you push the cart?"

Gordon was ready with a reply... "She said that if I behaved myself, I could pick out my own cereal."

Annie chuckled lightly under her breath and started again toward the porch.

"He was waitin' for ya', James," she mumbled. "Not bad."

"Yeah, yeah," he said, following beside her. "Could've been better."

"Could've been worse," said Annie.

James and Annie were settled in on the porch, seated in their assigned chairs, when Gordon came out of the house, leaving Carol to put the groceries away. He walked to the top of the steps, leaned against the post, looked out at the mid-morning sky.

"How was your trip?" asked James.

"Most satisfactory," said Gordon.

"Carol looks to have gotten comfortable in the neighborhood," said Annie. "Good to see."

"Absolutely," Gordon agreed.

"Well," James, struggling to hide a grin. "She just about meets the minimum age requirement."

Gordon ignored that last. Nothing worse than realizing your children are at the north end of middle-age, except maybe when they start complaining about getting old.

Wait a sec while I wipe this tear from my cheek...

"Either of you been to a store lately?" he asked, redirecting the conversation.

"Of course not," said James.

"You should check it out. They're all Christmased up. Overload, much? And not just department stores. I mean, you should see the grocery store." Gordon looked back at his friends. "And the music. You know I like holiday music, but jeez, tone it down a click."

He turned back to the view, sighed and slowly shook his head.

"Just a click," he grumbled.

"The Holiday season can be tough," said James, sympathetically.

Gordon's first Christmas without Jan...

"Yeah, well." Gordon gave another long sigh.

Gordon went into his office right after lunch, and had been hard at work all afternoon. He leaned back in his chair now, frowned at the monitor.

There was a quiet knock at the door. Gordon ignored it, gave the monitor a darker frown. Another knock at the door, the door slowly opened and Carol came in.

"Dad?"

Gordon leaned forward, ran through a few more keystrokes, looked away from the screen and leaned back again, looked up at Carol.

"Yeah?"

"You've been in here for hours." She glanced about the room before focusing on Gordon's desk, nodding to the computer monitor. "Are you going to tell me what you're working on?"

Gordon looked from his daughter to the monitor, considered, straightened in his chair.

"No secret, Carol," he said.

"So, maybe you can let me in on it, then?"

Gordon leaned forward just enough to reach out and maneuver the mouse, click and close the app. He shifted the chair about and looked up at Carol, smiled, drifted into thought, smiled again.

"A book," he said, matter-of-factly, giving a shrug.

Carol raised a questioning brow, as in... *give a little more, maybe?*

"A novel," said Gordon. "I'm putting together some of your mom and my adventures into a story."

"Really? That sounds great, Dad," said Carol. "Like, an autobiography?"

"Kind of a fictional memoir, I guess. Our story, your mom and me, framed within our adventures." He looked over at the computer monitor, now gone gray. "Fiction, but our story, put out there to remind the future that at one time in the past, we existed. We were here."

Carol looked down at her father, sitting there in his desk chair, in his cluttered office, looking faintly uncomfortable.

"I like it," she said.

Gordon gave another awkward shrug. He folded his arms across his chest then and looked pointedly up at his daughter.

"Okay. Your turn," he said. "You gonna tell me what *you're* working on?"

"I don't know what you mean."

Gordon gave a long, silent stare.

He could wait.

"All right, all right," she groaned. "A few lunches, a few walks, nothing more."

"Nothing?"

"Nothing," she stated, quite firmly. "It's not going anywhere. We're just friends. Really."

"Oh," said Gordon. "Too bad. Sorry, Carol."

"I wasn't looking for anything, Dad. He's nice, we have lunch now and again. Don't make more of it than there is."

"Hey, I'm just asking for James," said Gordon, grinning. "He was curious."

"Uh, huh." Carol hesitated, pursed her lips and curled her brow. "I see."

"Is he a doctor?" Gordon asked then. "James was wondering."

"Are my relationships a frequent topic of discussion?"

"Now and again." Another shrug, a long pause, another grin. "So. Any other news I can take back to the group? Something I can put on the agenda?"

Carol couldn't help but return the grin.

"Well... if you must, I had actually considered buying Kate's house."

"Really?" This took Gordon by surprise.

"But it sold so quick, I didn't get a chance to decide, one way or the other."

"Wow." The whole idea had come on so sudden he didn't know what he thought about it. Carol moving out?

Still, not to let it show. A quick redirect...

"So you'll have to wait for another of us to pass away then," he said.

"God, Dad. Don't be ghoulish."

"Right. Yeah, sorry 'bout that."

Carol gave him another frown, then gave a nod to the door.

"C'mon," she said. "Help me finish making dinner."

Gordon glanced up at the wall clock, back to Carol, already out the door and into the hall.

"Right," standing, rolling the chair under the desk. "Sure thing. On it."

Chapter Eight

The rain had been coming down rather heavy for most of the morning, creating a shifting sheen on the road. It had been raining off and on for several days, was forecast to continue for at least another day.

Gordon and Carol were sitting on the porch, hot cocoa in hand, taking in the dull drone of the rain on the porch roof.

Gordon took another long swig of the cocoa.

Not bad. Pretty good, actually. Carol had made it. She was getting better at it. Not as good as Jan used to make, but better than he could make.

Movement out on street caught Gordon's attention. He shifted position, looked through the thick shower of rain. It was coming down harder now, creating a cloud of mist as it struck asphalt.

It was Lloyd Weaver. He wore a hooded orange raincoat, his wooden staff in hand.

"Now that's what I call dedication," said Gordon.

"Obsession, you ask me," said Carol. "Even your Hole in the Wall Gang is staying under cover."

They watched Lloyd continue past. Gordon took another sip of his cocoa.

"When someone looks at Lloyd, looks at me, looks at any of us really, what do you think they see?"

"Um, I don't know," said Carol, uncertainly.

"They see an old person."

"Dad, I'm sorry to have to be the one to tell you..."

"Of course, Carol. But, you know what I see when I look at Lloyd? I see Lloyd and Suzy as a young couple moving into the neighborhood." Gordon gave a nod in the general direction of James' house. "I look at James, I don't see a grumpy old codger. I see a grumpy young codger. When I look at Annie, I see a vibrant young couple. Manny was always so alive."

"I remember," said Carol. "What's up, Dad?"

"Not sure. It's just..." Gordon considered. "Old folks weren't always old. We're not the snapshot in time that people see when they look at us. We have history."

"Some folks more history than others," she managed to say.

Gordon gave a warm smile at that, took another swallow of his cocoa.

"You know, it was Lloyd and Suzy who first got your mom and me started on going on adventures and not simply vacations."

Carol recalled her dad saying something along those lines more than once over the years. She mumbled an *I know* in answer.

"You know there's a mountain trail hiking trip in Europe that takes you through three countries."

"Really?" Carol had actually heard that story all her life.

"It was our first adventure. We went as a foursome."

"It must have been amazing."

"That it was," wistfully. He fell silent for a long moment, then, "I know I'm eighty years old, Carol; going on eighty-one. But... I'm not." He held his free hand to his chest, over his heart. "Not in here. Okay, I may not be twenty any more..."

He had no end to that sentence. He looked into his cup, took the last swallow of his cocoa. He held the cup in his lap, looked out into the neighborhood.

"For all the world out there, we're just a street of old folks," he said.

"Like it or not," said Carol. "I'll be with you soon enough."

"Having a daughter as old as you doesn't help my argument any."

"Tough." Carol took her own last swallow from her cocoa.

Rocky made an appearance then, working his way along the yards across the street, taking care of his morning business. Rain or no rain.

"Mom loved days like this," Carol said then.

Next morning; breakfast was out of the way, dishes were in the dishwasher, Gordon's coffee cup had been rinsed out and was sitting on the counter next to the coffee maker, awaiting its next use. Gordon left the kitchen just as Carol came from the hallway carrying a box with "Christmas" written on the side.

The living room was already covered with holiday decorations, with very little room for much more.

Carol was actually a few days late getting started... Jan always began the decorating the day after Thanksgiving.

"I think there's an empty spot over by the stereo," said Gordon, appreciating his own humor.

"Got it. I'm on it," said Carol, setting the box on the couch, not taking the bait.

Gordon continued across the living room and went out onto the porch. He found James already there, sitting in his chair at the end of the row. Gordon gave him a half-nod, continued to the top step and stood looking out, taking in the morning.

James looked briefly in Gordon's direction, then forward.

"I took the test," he said, quite matter-of-factly.

"Right..." said Gordon, nodding slowly. "And what test would that be?"

"John took me in. The doctor gave me some kind of prelim test. Some test to see if they have need go deeper."

"Right..." Gordon turned about and went over to his chair. He sat with a groan, gave a mumbled "Sooo?".

"Dementia test," said James. "I told John about our talk, he thought why not go check it out."

"Ah. Right. So?"

"You know, just to ease my mind."

"Yeah. What's left of it," growled Gordon. "James..." prompting.

"The doctor says I'm fine. Not to worry."

A few moments of quiet on the porch.

"That's great, James," said Gordon then, calmly, sincerely.

"That it is," said James.

Rocky made his appearance then, working his way along the yards across the street.

"A bit late," said James.

"Not really," said Gordon.

There was another movement then, further up the street, to their left.

Lloyd?

No. It was Annie. She was working her way along the middle of the street, pushing her walker out in front of her. She came nearer, nearer. To all appearances, it looked as though the walker was becoming a hindrance more than a benefit.

Gordon and James watched as she carefully made her way from the street and onto the lawn. Neither Gordon nor James made any attempt to get up from their chairs.

"What do you think you're doing, Annie?" asked Gordon. "You shoulda called."

"I'm fine." Annie reached the bottom step, looked up at her friends. "I appreciate your concern."

She set the walker aside, held onto the rail and climbed the steps. Gordon and James watched as she worked her way over to her chair. Gordon turned then and looked out at the neighborhood.

"Imagine the flack we'd take if you took a tumble in the street and we weren't there to pick you up."

"Sorry," said Annie, settling in. "I don't know what I was thinking."

"All right, then. I forgive you."

"Hmmph..." said James.

With that all settled, all fell silent. Gordon leaned back in his chair, gave it another few moments. He gave a nod then, raised a hand and tapped his chin with a raised finger.

"So, I heard through the grapevine... that major holiday that we talked about recently... it's coming up soon," he said.

"I heard the same," said Annie. "I understand that it happens most every year."

"That would explain the giant tree in my living room," said James.

They heard the sound of the small convoy before they saw it, watched then as it entered the neighborhood and slowly passed by. A sedan led the way, followed by a pickup with the truck bed fully loaded and tarped over, finally then a mid-size moving van bringing up the rear.

"That's it, then. There goes the neighborhood," said James.

"Don't be mean," said Annie.

The mini-convoy continued on down the street.

The new neighbors are moving in.

"They might be perfectly nice people," said Gordon.

"No doubt," said James.

Gordon stood, stepped over to the top step. He rested a hand on the post, then leaned out and looked up the street in the direction of the newly-arriving neighbors.

Activity just visible from the porch, vehicles positioning themselves...

Gordon straightened up and looked back over his shoulder. James and Annie were leaning near one another, were in quiet conversation. A smile, a nod, a light chuckle.

Watching his friends, it seemed to Gordon that they were very much of the neighborhood. The neighborhood would be less without them, they much less without the neighborhood.

He turned about then, pushed off from the post, took the steps down into the yard; he walked out into the yard, stopped. He stuffed his hands into his pockets.

"You going somewhere?" called James.

Gordon considered. The question was more complicated than James realized.

"Not sure." He glanced back then to his friends up on the porch. James was looking down in his direction, a curious expression. He said something to Annie. Annie commented, they each nodded, returned to their conversation.

Gordon turned back to the neighborhood.

Not sure... he thought to himself.

He had been trying for weeks to come up with a suitable adventure for the three of them, some brief trip they could take come late Spring, maybe Summer. He was having a tough time of it. James insisted that any vacation/trip be something that "old folks like us" could handle. And of course Annie might still be in some manner of late-stage recovery.

And then, their three personalities and interests were rather dissimilar. Not like he and Jan. Suggestions had often been met with "sounds exhausting" or "eh" or a silent shoulder-shrug.

All right, then. More and more clear then... Gordon's friends were less than enthusiastic about any adventure that might take them more than a mile or two from the neighborhood.

So then... Go on his own?

Really?

More to the point, an adventure without Jan?

Maybe that had been the problem all along. Maybe it had nothing to do with friends who were not all that eager to go climb a mountain or ride the rapids at their age.

Maybe Gordon didn't want to go without Jan.

So, what then? Maybe some occasional local outings, just to keep the blood flowing?

They had tried a bingo night at the nearby senior center. That hadn't gone well at all. James hated it, Annie gave her "eh" shoulder-shrug, and Gordon won a cheese basket.

It was a very nice cheese basket.

So, not to surrender, not to give up...

An idea then. The more he thought on it... he turned half-about, looked up at the porch. He gave a *hey* to get their attention.

"You still here?" asked James.

"A block party," Gordon stated.

"Huh?"

"We have a block party."

"We already have a block party," said Annie.

"Yeah," agreed James.

"It's called the James' Thanksgiving Backyard Block Party," said Annie. "I missed it this year. Heard it was great."

"Not the same thing," said Gordon. Looking forward again. "This Summer. We block off the street at both ends, have a neighborhood block party, the whole street."

"Well..." James considered.

"We can do that?" asked Annie. "Do we need to get a permit?"

"So, we get a permit."

James continued to consider. "Fourth of July," he said... considering.

"Fourth of July," stated Gordon. There was silence of acceptance from the two on the porch. "We'll do it then."

"This summer..." said Annie, both a statement and a question.

"This Summer," Gordon stated; with finality.

"So then, Gordon. You still gonna do some global adventure thing?" asked James.

Well that put the nail in the old oblong box. Gordon noted that James hadn't included himself in any adventure.

"Not sure. Still thinkin' on it," he said, hardly above a whisper. He took a few more steps toward the street. He glanced out, at the homes, the yards, the wide asphalt avenue.

It was comforting to Gordon. It was his world, his home. Wherever he might go, whatever adventures he might have.. this was home.

Back behind him, on his porch, his friends. He looked back over his shoulder. James and Annie were sitting in their chairs. They were leaning near one another, in quiet conversation, occasionally glancing in his direction. Behind them, in the house, Gordon's home these decades gone by, his daughter was decorating for the upcoming holiday.

Christmas... calendar's way of calling attention to another year gone past, looking ahead to the year to come.

Always a concern for Gordon, and often called attention to by James: *another year gone.*

Still, it was always great to still be around for the next, as Gordon often had to remind James. It was certainly better than the alternative.

And to experience those years here, on this street, in this neighborhood. His neighborhood.

Gordon turned fully about, looked up at the porch.

His porch. His and Jan's.

He gave a warm smile at those on his porch, James and Annie. As much their porch as his, really. Theirs and those no longer here. Together they had shared the decades, shared the experiences, experienced the world through the curtain of the neighborhood.

From the porch.

A sudden thought then, coming from nowhere in particular.

“A safari,” he stated. “A photo safari.”

Conversation stopped. James and Annie looked down at Gordon.

“So, like a safari with cameras?” asked Annie. “Rather than with guns?”

“Right. Exactly.”

Gordon waited, watched those on the porch for some further acknowledgment of the suggestion.

James then, tentatively, “Um, how long would we gave to be gone?”

Have to be gone...

Really?

Gordon frowned, grumbled a low grumble.

He turned back again to the neighborhood.

“Right, right...”

The sun was shining, the day warming.

Yep. It's gonna be a nice day...

End Gordon's Porch Two
Book 2 of the serial

www.ingramcontent.com/pod-product-compliance
Lightning Source LLC
LaVergne TN
LVHW050946080826
845145LV00004B/1423

* 9 7 8 0 9 9 8 7 5 3 5 6 0 *